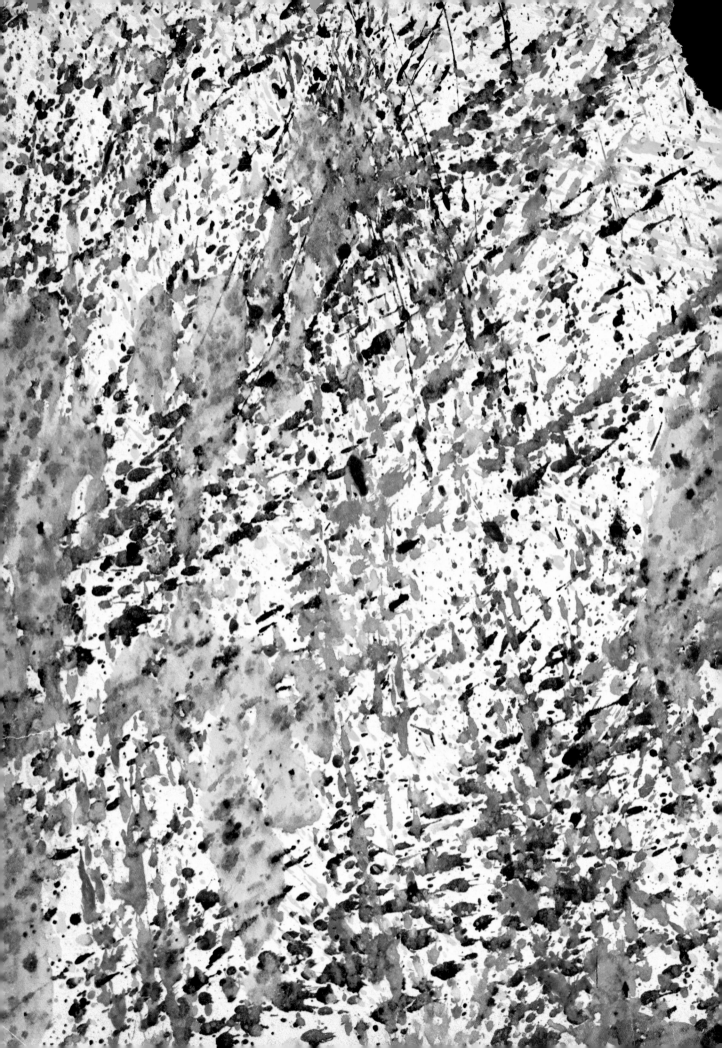

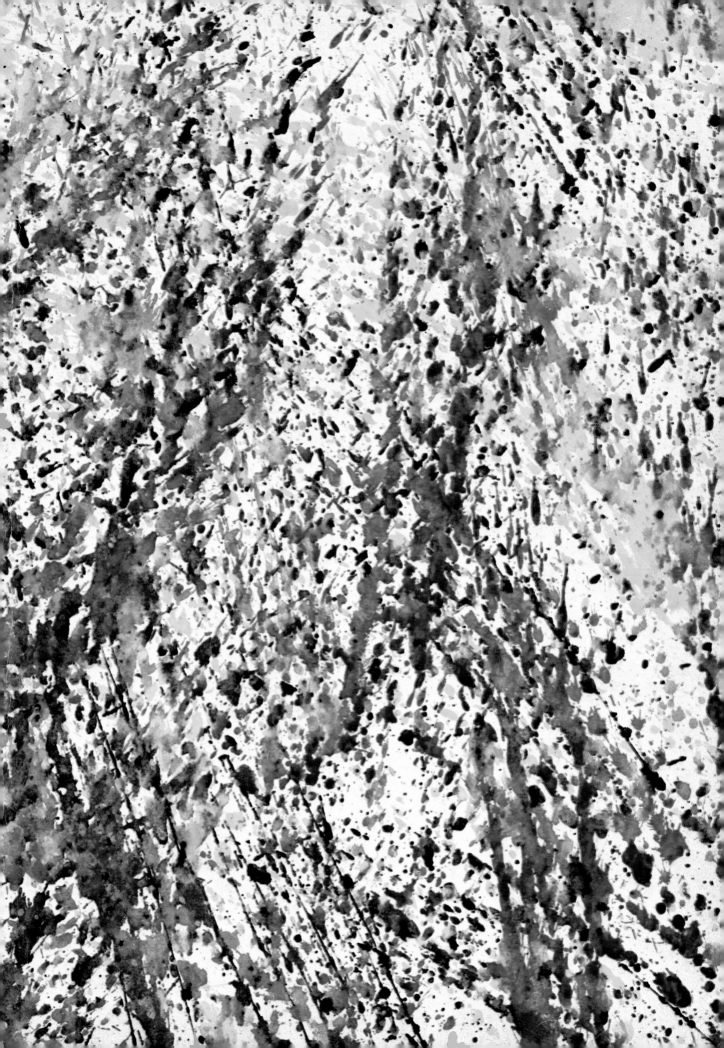

Eric Carle's Storybook

Seven Tales by the Brothers Grimm

illustrated and retold by Eric Carle

FRANKLIN WATTS · NEW YORK · LONDON · 1976

Published in 1976 by Franklin Watts, Inc.
730 Fifth Avenue, New York, N.Y. 10019

All rights reserved
Library of Congress Catalog Card Number: 75–44951
SBN (trade edition): 531–02436–9
SBN (library edition): 531–01050–3

Printed in Italy

Contents

Hans in Luck

Hans had worked seven years with a miller and he felt it was time to go home.

"Seven years have passed, and that is long enough," he said to his master one morning. "I would like to see my mother. Please give me my wages, and I'll be on my way."

"Hans," said the miller, "you have been a good and faithful worker. My wife and I shall miss you, but we wish you the best of luck and a safe trip home."

The miller went to his strongbox and took out Hans's wages. "Here is your pay," he said, and gave Hans a piece of gold the size of his head.

Hans wrapped the gold inside a sack, and threw it over his shoulder. He took his walking stick in his hand, crossed the bridge to the road, and started on his way home.

The road was rough and hilly, and the midmorning sun was hot. Hans began to sweat. The gold seemed very heavy indeed. Just then a horseman came galloping by.

"Ah," said Hans, "a horse is a fine thing. A horseman does not have to carry a heavy load like mine on his back."

"What is in your sack?" asked the horseman.

"It is a piece of gold, and it is quite a lump to carry," said Hans.

"If you like, we will trade," said the horseman. "I will give you the horse and you will give me the gold."

"A good deal," said Hans.

The man helped Hans onto the horse, then made off with the gold as fast as he could. Hans went on his way, feeling lucky to be riding along so easily. But the horse soon understood that Hans was no rider, and Hans was thrown to the ground. A farmer milking his cow in a nearby field stopped the horse and helped Hans to his feet.

Hans was very thirsty. "Dear man," he said to the farmer, "it must be wonderful to have milk whenever you want some. And good fresh butter and cheese, besides. How I would like to have a cow."

"A cow is indeed a very fine thing," replied the farmer, "but a horse can be useful too. If you like, I will trade my cow for your horse."

"A good deal," said Hans. "A horse is not for me. I will never ride that animal again. A cow will suit me better." He took the cow, and the farmer climbed onto the horse and rode away in a great hurry.

Hans felt he was the luckiest man in the world, and he sat down to milk his cow. But milking a cow was something he had never done before and he was clumsy at it. He pushed and pinched and pulled, but the cow would give no milk. Hans tried again, twice as hard. At last the cow became impatient. She raised one of her hind legs and gave Hans a good kick.

Just then it happened that a man was passing by on the road. He had a big fat pig, which he was taking to market.

"Why should the cow kick you?" asked the man.

Hans told of his troubles. "The cow looks poorly," said the man. "Maybe she doesn't give much milk."

"What!" said Hans. "How much better if I had a lovely fat pig like yours. Pork chops and roasts, to say nothing of sausages."

"Well," said the man, "just for you, I'll trade. You take the pig and I'll take the cow."

The exchange was made and Hans set out again. But the pig was stubborn. No matter how much Hans wanted to go one way, the pig wanted to go the other way. Besides, it squealed and screeched and grunted like — well, just like a pig.

Hans was getting discouraged when a woman with a fat goose walked by.

"Eggs for breakfast," Hans thought, "and feathers for a pillow, and a roast for Christmas, all from one bird. Not bad. Perhaps the woman is willing to trade."

The woman knew a good bargain when she saw one and was happy to trade. Hans went on and was close to home when he saw a knife grinder at work. What fun! Sparks were flying through the air, and the grinder's money pouch was full of coins.

"That's a fine goose you have," said the grinder. "Where did you buy it?"

"It was a lucky swap," said Hans, and he told the grinder of all his trades, starting with the lump of gold.

"You've a good head for business," said the grinder. "You should take up my work."

"How can I do that?" said Hans. "I have no grindstone."

"Well," said the grinder, as he picked up a loose cobblestone from the road. "It so happens that I have an extra one. I'll trade it, just for the goose." And so they traded a goose for the old cobblestone.

Hans felt he was the luckiest man in the world. But he had walked a long way and he was very tired and thirsty. The stone grew heavier and heavier every minute. At last he came to a water fountain. He put the stone at the fountain's edge and bent over to take a drink. The stone rolled over and sank deep into the water with a loud *plump.*

Hans laughed. "How lucky I am," he said. "Now I am free, with nothing at all to carry anymore." And he ran home, where his mother saw him coming and rushed to greet him.

"Oh, Hans, how I have missed you," said his mother. "How wonderful it is to have you home again."

She gave him a big, warm hug and led him to the most comfortable chair in the house so that he could sit and rest. Then she bustled around, telling him all the village news while she prepared his favorite supper, a dish of steaming dumplings. Now, more than ever, Hans felt that he was the luckiest young man in the world.

The Three Golden Hairs

Once upon a time a beautiful little girl was born to a poor man and his wife. A wise old woman in the village saw the baby and said, "This child is specially blessed. She will always be lucky and when she is eighteen, she will be queen of the land."

It happened that the real queen heard about the prophecy. She became fearful and thought, "I am the queen — there can be no other." Then she put on a disguise and traveled through the country to the village where the blessed child was born.

She went to the poor man and his wife and said in a friendly way, "Give me your child and I will raise her with great care." The woman offered them a bag of gold and the poor parents gave up their luck-child, believing that no real harm could ever come to her.

But the queen threw the baby into the nearest river. "Good riddance," she said, thinking the child would surely drown.

Instead, the baby floated gently down the river to a mill. There the miller saw the bundle with the child and pulled it from the water. The good miller and his wife were delighted with the little girl and raised her as their own daughter. She was a kind, clever child, and they blessed the day that they found her.

Eighteen years later the queen was traveling by on her way to a great ball in the next kingdom. Just as she came to the mill, a thunderstorm broke loose and she took shelter inside. The miller and his wife were honored to have the queen in their house, and they had their adopted child serve her tea.

"Is this lovely girl your daughter?" asked the queen.

"We think of her as our daughter, even though she is not our own," said the miller. "Eighteen years ago I pulled her from the water, when she was only a baby."

At once the queen realized that this was the very child whom she thought she had drowned. She wanted to get rid of the girl. "Could your daughter take a letter to the king for me?" she asked.

"It would be our honor," replied the miller.

"Dear King," she wrote. "When this young woman arrives at the castle, kill her at once, for she is a wicked witch. From your Queen." She sealed the letter and gave it to the girl, who started on her way to the king.

The journey was long, and when darkness fell the girl became lost in the forest. After many hours of wandering she saw a light in a house. She knocked at the door and an old woman opened it. "This is a robbers' house," the old woman said. "Go away before they come home and do you harm."

"I must deliver a letter to the king," said the young woman. "I am lost and tired. Please help me."

The old woman was curious about the letter, so she took the girl in and fed her and put her to bed. When the robbers returned, at first they were angry with the old woman. Then they too became curious about the letter. They opened it and read it.

"That queen is tricking this young woman," said the leader. "Let's fix the mean old thing." He sat down and wrote another letter.

"Dear King," he wrote. "When this young woman arrives at the castle, marry her to our son. Do not wait for my return. From your Queen."

The leader burned the first letter and put the second in its place as the young woman slept. In the morning she thanked her hosts and left for the castle, where she delivered the robbers' letter.

The king thought it strange that the queen would not want to be at the prince's wedding. "But she must have her reasons," he thought, and he had the marriage performed.

When the queen returned, she saw that her plan had gone wrong and she decided to get rid of the new princess in some other way.

"You must prove to me that you truly love my son," she said to the young woman. "Go find the devil and bring back three golden hairs from his beard."

The princess took a horse and wagon and started out. Soon she came to a town, where the guard asked her, "Who are you and what do you know?"

"I know everything," answered the princess.

"Then tell me why our fountain, which used to pour forth red wine, now doesn't even give water," said the guard.

"I shall tell you when I return," said the princess.

At the next town the guard asked her, "Who are you and what do you know?"

"I know everything," said the princess.

"Then tell me why our apple tree, which used to bear golden apples, now doesn't even have leaves," said the guard.

"I shall tell you when I return," said the princess.

At last she came to a river and asked the ferryman to take her across. "Who are you and what do you know?" he said.

"I know everything," replied the princess.

"Then tell me why I must ferry back and forth, back and forth, and never be relieved," said the ferryman.

"I shall tell you when I return," answered the princess.

After a while she came to the devil's house. He was not at home, but his grandmother greeted her. "You are so young and beautiful," said the grandmother. "Go away or the devil will harm you."

"I have come to get three golden hairs from his beard, and I have three questions to ask," said the princess. She told her questions to the old woman.

"In that case, stay," said the grandmother. "But I shall have to use my magic to hide you from the devil." She thought for a moment, then changed the princess into an owl. "Now just sit here and keep your ears open," she said.

The devil came home and had a big meal. Then, as usual,

he sat down to drink some coffee and listen to his grandmother's tales. They made him sleepy. Soon he began to snore.

Quickly the grandmother pulled a golden hair from his chin. "Ow," cried the devil. "What is it?" "I dreamed about a fountain. It used to give red wine, but not anymore. Why?" asked the grandmother. "Because a toad sits at the bottom of the fountain," said the devil, and he fell asleep.

Soon the grandmother pulled a second golden hair from his chin. "Ow," cried the devil. "What is it?" "I dreamed about an apple tree. It used to bear golden apples, but not anymore. Why?" said the grandmother. "Because a mouse is eating one of its roots," said the devil, and he fell asleep.

Then the grandmother pulled a third golden hair from his chin. "Ow," cried the devil. "What is it now?" "I dreamed about a ferryman. He goes back and forth and no one ever relieves him. What should he do?" said the grandmother. "Give the oar to the next passenger and run," said the devil. "Now leave me alone or I'll — I'll — " and he fell asleep again.

In the morning, when the devil had left, the grandmother turned the owl back to a young princess and gave her the golden hairs. "Leave quickly," she said. "You have the answers."

After the ferryman had taken the young woman across the river, she said, "Give your next passenger the oar and run."

At the town with the apple tree and the town with the fountain, she told the guards the answers to their questions. When the people of the towns found that she was right, they each gave her a sack of gold. So the lucky princess returned home not only with the three golden hairs from the devil, but also with two sacks of gold.

The prince was delighted to see his bride. She gave the three golden hairs to the queen, who was still determined to get rid of the young woman. But at the moment she was more interested in the gold, for she was very greedy.

"Where did you get all that gold, dear?" she asked the princess.

"I crossed the river on a ferry. On the farther shore, gold lies like sand. I scooped this up," said the princess.

"Can I get some too?" asked the queen.

"As much as you like. Just take the ferry," said the princess.

The queen started out. It was cold and rainy when she came to the ferry. "No time to waste. Row me across the river quickly," she said to the ferryman.

He took her to the other shore, then placed the oar in her hand and ran away. And there the queen has been rowing back and forth, back and forth, ever since.

So, since the old queen had disappeared, things happened just as the wise old village woman had predicted eighteen years before. The princess became queen. She was just and generous to her people and they loved her. The old queen had been hated by everyone. No one missed her at all and no one ever tried to find out what had become of her.

The Fisherman
and His Wife

There was once a poor fisherman who lived with his wife in a tiny hut by the sea. Each morning he went down to the shore and cast his net for fish. One day he pulled up a fish with gold and silver scales. "Oh," said the fish, "I beg you to let me go. I am really an enchanted prince, and not at all good to eat."

"Prince or no prince, any fish who can talk has earned its freedom," said the fisherman, and he let the fish go.

When he told his wife what had happened, she said, "You nincompoop, that was a magic fish, the kind that makes wishes come true. You should have made a wish."

"But we have everything we need," said the fisherman.

His wife did not listen. "Tomorrow," she said, "catch the fish again and ask it for a big house like those in the city. And I'd like a black dress with white frills, too."

The fisherman did not like to oppose his wife so he cast his net in the same place the next day. Little waves were beating against the shore. Soon he pulled up the fish. "What is it?" asked the fish with the silver and gold scales.

refrain

"My wife says I should have made a wish," said the fisherman. "She wants a big house like those in the city, and a black dress with white frills."

"Go home," said the fish. "She has them already."

The fisherman went home. Sure enough, his wife, in a black dress with white frills, stood in front of a big house.

A week passed, and the fisherman's wife began to find the house too small. "Go find the magic fish," she said. "I want to be a queen and live in a castle."

"But surely now we have everything we need," said the fisherman.

"I must be queen," his wife kept saying. Finally the fisherman gave in and went to the water.

The water along the shore was black, and the wind was high. The fisherman said to the fish when it appeared, "My wife wants to be queen and live in a castle."

"Go home," said the fish. "She already has her wish."

The fisherman went home and, indeed, his wife was now a queen. She stood at the door of a splendid big castle.

"Ah," said the fisherman. "Now you are queen. There is nothing more you can want."

"I am not satisfied with being queen," said his wife. "Go to the fish and tell it I want to be pope."

"Oh, no," said the fisherman. "This time you are asking too much. I do not want to go."

But in the end he went to find the fish. The waves were as high as mountains, and the sky was black. In fright, the fisherman said, "My wife now wants to be pope."

"Go home," said the fish. "She has her wish."

The fisherman went home and found a great church decorated in gold. Tall candles burned before his wife, who was dressed in a pope's robes.

"Now surely you cannot wish for anything more," he said.

"I will think about it," replied his wife. That night she could not sleep, thinking of what else she might be. She got up early, just as the sun was rising. "Ah," she thought, "I should like to be the one who makes the sun rise."

She awoke her husband. "Go to the fish," she commanded. "Tell it I want to make the sun rise. I want to be ruler of the universe."

In terror, the fisherman went to the shore. A wild storm was raging. "Oh, fish," shouted the fisherman above the noise of the wind, "my wife wants to be ruler of the universe."

"Go home," said the fish. And the fisherman went home. He found his wife dressed in her old clothes inside their little hut.

For the rest of their lives the fisherman and his wife lived in the little hut by the sea. Every day the fisherman went to the shore and cast his net. As the years went by, he pulled up hundreds of fish, but never again did he see the magic gold- and silver-scaled fish who could talk and grant wishes.

Tom Thumb

A poor woodcutter sat by the fire one evening, while his wife sat across from him, spinning. He said, "What a sad thing it is that we have no children. We live too quietly. A child would cheer us up."

"Yes," said his wife. "I'd even be glad of one the size of my thumb."

Some time later they had a son, and sure enough, he was no bigger than a thumb. They named him Tom Thumb, and they loved him dearly and gave him the best of care.

Time passed. Tom never grew any larger, but he was strong and healthy. He became a quick, bright child who did well at whatever he tried.

One morning, when his father was getting ready to go into the forest to cut some wood, he said, "I wish I had someone to bring me the horse and cart later on."

"Leave the horse to me," said Tom. "I can bring him."

"Very well," replied his father.

That afternoon Tom climbed up and sat between the horse's ears. "Gittup," he called to the horse in a big brave voice, and away they went together.

Two strangers were passing through the wood and saw the horse galloping. They heard Tom calling to it to turn right or left, but there was no one to be seen. "That's very strange," they said. "Let's follow the cart and see what happens when it stops."

Soon the men came to the spot where Tom's father was waiting, and they hid behind a tree. "Here I am, Father," Tom called. "Didn't I drive the horse well?"

"Yes, you're a fine boy," said the woodcutter, as he lifted Tom to his shoulder.

"We could make a fortune with that odd little fellow," said one of the men. "If we showed him in the towns for money, people would pay to see him. Let's buy him."

"Hey, there," he said to the woodcutter. "Here's a fine piece of gold. Sell us the boy. We'll take good care of him."

"No," said the woodcutter. "He is all my wife and I have, and we love him with all our hearts."

But Tom whispered in his father's ear, "Take the gold and don't worry about me. I'll be home before you know it."

"Well, all right then," said the woodcutter, and he took the gold.

One of the men put Tom on the rim of his hat and they all said their good-byes. Tom's father went one way with the horse and the wood and the piece of gold. The two men went the other way with Tom riding on the hat.

After a while, Tom called, "Let me down."

"No," said the men. "You'll just run away."

"But it's important business," said Tom.

So the men put Tom down in the grass. Quick as a wink he ran into a mouse hole. "Good-bye, gentlemen," he called.

The men looked everywhere, but they could not see Tom. They poked in the hole, but he stayed safely out of reach. "We've been tricked," they said angrily, and they went on their way.

When Tom came out of the hole, the moon was up. "Traveling at night is risky," Tom said. So he curled up in a snail shell that lay in the field nearby.

Just as he was falling asleep, he heard two men passing by.

"That rich man has gold and silver and jewels, but how can we get in to steal them?" asked one man.

"I can help you," shouted Tom.

"Whose voice is that? Where are you?" asked the thieves.

"Here. In the grass."

When the thieves saw Tom, they laughed.

"How could a little fellow like you help us?" they said.

"I could slip into the house and hand out to you whatever you want," said Tom.

"All right, it's worth a try," said the thieves. "Come along."

But when Tom got inside the house, he called out in a loud voice, "What do you want? Shall I hand out everything?"

"S-sh," said the thieves. "Not so loud."

Tom pretended not to understand.

"Hold out your hands," he shouted. "Here's some gold."

The maid heard the noise and came with a lamp. Quickly the thieves ran away, and Tom, pleased with himself, tiptoed out to the barn. There he went to sleep in a pile of soft hay, thinking he'd be home in time for dinner the next day. In the morning the maid came to feed the cow. She picked up the pile of hay where Tom was sleeping. When he woke up, he was in the cow's mouth. The cow swallowed, and Tom slid into her stomach. He screamed, but the maid had already left to do the baking.

Later the maid came back to milk the cow. Imagine her surprise when she heard a voice inside it, crying, "Let me out. Let me out."

She ran to her master. "The cow is talking," she said.

Her master came to listen. Again a voice called, "Let me out. Let me out."

The master turned pale with fright. "It's an evil spirit," he said. "We must kill the cow."

So he butchered the cow and threw her stomach into the rubbish heap, with Tom still inside. Tom twisted and turned, trying to work his way out of the stomach. Just as he was beginning to sniff fresh air a starving wolf came by. The wolf pounced on the stomach and gulped it down — but still Tom did not lose courage.

"Dear friend," called Tom from inside the wolf, "I know where you can find the most delicious food."

"Where is that?" asked the wolf.

"The woodcutter's house," said Tom. "I'll tell you how to get there."

When they came to the house, Tom said, "Go to the narrow window in the back, and force yourself through. That's where the pantry is."

The wolf pushed his way through the narrow window and ate until he was stuffed full. But when he tried to leave, his stomach had grown so big and fat he could not get out.

Now Tom began to scream as loud as he could, "Help, help!"

"Be quiet," said the wolf. "You'll awake everyone up." But Tom kept on screaming.

Before long, the woodcutter and his wife heard the noise and came with an ax. Upon seeing the wolf, the woodcutter shouted, "I'll get you, you thief!" And he swung the ax back for the kill.

"Father, Father!" yelled Tom. "I'm in the wolf's belly."

"Don't worry, I won't hurt you," the woodcutter replied, and he struck the wolf dead with one blow on its head. Then he cut the wolf open and took Tom out. "Thank heaven you're back," he said. "Where on earth have you been?"

"I've been seeing the world," said Tom. "Now I am happy to breathe the fresh air again. I've been inside a mouse hole, a snail shell, a cow's stomach, and a wolf's belly. And now I'll stay right here with you."

"And we will never give you away again for all the gold in the world," said his parents, as they hugged and kissed their child.

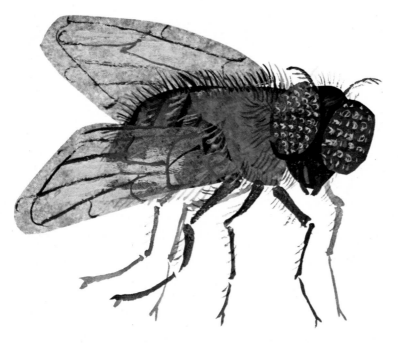

Seven with One Blow

One summer morning a tailor was sitting on his bench by the window and feeling very pleased with himself, for he was sewing a new suit for the mayor. Looking out at the village street, he saw a farm woman with a basket coming his way. She was calling, "Jams and jellies for sale. Jams and jellies for sale. Fine grape jelly, delicious grape jelly, only a penny a spoonful."

"That sounds wonderful," said the tailor to himself. "It's almost lunchtime and I'm hungry. Grape jelly would be just the right thing to go with that fresh loaf of bread in the cupboard."

He put his head out the window and called to the woman, "Come over here. I'll buy some of your jelly."

The woman came in through the door. "I'll take a spoonful," said the tailor, handing her a penny. After she had gone, he cut a slice of bread and put the jelly on it. "I'll just finish stitching this seam before I eat," he said.

He laid the bread and jelly down and went on sewing as fast as he could. But soon a great swarm of flies began buzzing around his meal. Some of them even landed on it.

"Who invited you?" asked the tailor, shooing the flies away. But they only circled in the air and came right back. Finally they made the tailor angry. He picked up a piece of cloth and hit at them with all his strength. When he looked he saw that he had killed seven flies in that one terrific blow.

"Look at that," he said. "I didn't know I was so strong. I must go out in the world. Tailoring is not for me."

He had a little money, and with it he bought a breastplate. Across the plate he printed in big, bold letters, SEVEN WITH ONE BLOW.

He stuffed a piece of soft cheese into one of his pockets, and into the other pocket he put his pet bird. Then he locked the door of his shop and started out on his journey.

He went along cheerfully until he came to the top of a high hill. Here a huge giant was sitting, looking at the world spread out below him.

"Good day, comrade," said the tailor. "Are you traveling, too? Perhaps we can journey together."

The giant looked at him scornfully. "Me? Travel with a little fellow like you?" he said. Then he caught sight of the tailor's breastplate. "There must be something to a person who can kill seven men with one blow," he went on, "but you must prove yourself." Then he picked up a rock and squeezed it until water dripped from it. "Let's see you do that," he said.

"Simple," said the tailor. He pretended to pick up a rock, but secretly pulled the cheese from his pocket. Then he squeezed the cheese until the whey dripped from it in big, steady drops.

The giant was more than a little surprised, but he still had his doubts about the tailor. "Let's see you do this," he said. He picked up another rock and threw it with all his might. It flew through the air and landed more than half a mile away.

"Easy," said the tailor. Again he pretended to pick up a rock, but at the same time he took the bird from his pocket. Then he threw the bird into the air. It was happy to be free and it flew higher and higher and farther and farther until at last it disappeared from sight.

The giant was astonished and he was frightened. He had never met a man who was stronger than himself. He looked again at the breastplate that said SEVEN WITH ONE BLOW, then he turned and ran away as fast as his big, strong legs could carry him.

The tailor traveled on from town to town until one day he came to the courtyard of a royal palace. He was tired and lay down to take a nap. While he was sleeping, people stopped to read the words on his breastplate. "Seven men with one blow," someone said and ran to tell the king. The king thought for a minute, then sent a messenger to ask the tailor to enter the royal army. "That is exactly why I am here," said the tailor.

The king was pleased and gave the tailor a fine house and many other gifts. But the other soldiers soon became jealous. They threatened to resign if the tailor remained. The king did not wish to lose all his faithful men for the sake of one, so he tried to get rid of the tailor. "There are two giants in the forest," he said. "They are ruining my kingdom. I will give you a bag of gold if you will kill them."

"Nothing to it," said the tailor.

In the forest the tailor found the two giants sleeping under a large tree. He hid behind a boulder and threw a stone on the nose of the first giant. The giant woke up and said to the second giant, "Hey, don't do that."

"What are you talking about?" said the second giant. "You must be dreaming."

They went back to sleep, and the tailor now threw a stone on the nose of the second giant. He woke up and screamed at the first giant, "Stop that, you birdbrain."

"Birdbrain, ha?" shouted the first giant.

"Dummkopf!" roared the second giant.

Soon they were kicking and punching and throwing rocks at each other. Finally they pulled up trees and clubbed each other to death. When the king's men came to see what had happened they found the tailor standing, sword in hand, by the two dead giants.

So the tailor earned his gold, and the king's daughter began to take a liking to him. "There's a unicorn in the mountains," she said. "If you can catch it, I'll marry you."

"Nothing to it," said the tailor.

He took a rope and an ax and went looking for the animal. Finally he found the creature, and the tailor, standing in front of a tree trunk, began to tease it. The unicorn scraped the ground with its hooves and snorted through its nostrils, but the tailor kept right on teasing.

At last the angry unicorn rushed at the tailor to pierce him through. But the nimble tailor jumped away, and the unicorn ran its horn right through the tree. It struggled for a long time, but in vain. Then the tailor tied his rope around its neck, chopped the unicorn loose, and led the exhausted creature to the palace.

So the tailor and the princess were married. Things went well, except that the tailor talked in his sleep. One night the princess heard him say, "Give me the piece of cloth and I'll make a beautiful dress for you." The next night she listened and he said, "How do you like the stitches?" Now she was certain that her husband was a tailor, and not a knight. She went to her father and told him what had happened. "Tonight, when you are both in bed, I shall send in three of my strongest men," said the king. "They will kill your husband."

By chance, the court jester heard the plan. He warned the tailor. When the men tiptoed into the bedroom, the tailor pretended to be asleep. Just as they raised their weapons he said, "I have killed seven with one blow, frightened off one giant, killed two other giants, and captured a wild unicorn. Why should I be afraid of the three ordinary soldiers who are now trying to kill me?"

When the three men heard the tailor, they ran out of the room and never were seen again.

From that time on, no one lifted a hand against the tailor, and no one dared offend him in any way. He was known far and wide as a hero and a warrior. When the old king died, the tailor who had begun his adventures by killing seven flies with one blow became the new ruler. And he governed the country wisely for the rest of his long, long life.

The Youth Who Wanted to Shiver

A father had two sons. Everyone agreed that the elder one was clever, and the younger one, Jack, was stupid. Yet when the father asked his elder son to go on an errand late at night that led past a scary place, the boy would say, "I can't go there. It makes me shiver. Send Jack." Or sometimes when people sat around the fireplace telling ghost stories, someone would say, "Oh, that makes me shiver." Jack would always wonder, "What does it mean to shiver?" Jack was never afraid.

One day Jack's father said, "Son, you must learn a trade."

"I want to learn to shiver," said Jack. "I would love to know that."

Jack's father told the village sexton of his troubles. "Send him to me," said the sexton. "I'll teach him to shiver." So Jack was sent to the sexton's home.

He told Jack to ring the bells in the church tower at midnight. Then he dressed in white sheets and stood on the stairs where Jack could see him. He moaned and he groaned so that the boy would think he was a ghost and would be afraid.

"Who are you?" asked Jack. "Speak up, if you have honest business here, or else go away. I must ring the bells."

"No-o-o, no-o-o," moaned the sexton.

"Oh, yes," said Jack, and he kicked the man downstairs. Then he rang the bells twelve times and went home to bed.

The next morning the sexton was found lying with many broken bones at the foot of the stairs. He blamed Jack's stupidity for his misfortune. Jack's father was afraid his son would give the family a bad name. He gave him some money and sent him away, saying, "I am sure that no one here will want to teach you how to shiver."

"Well," said Jack, "I'll try my luck somewhere else."

As he walked along the country road the next day, he kept mumbling, "If I only knew what it is to shiver."

By chance a man overheard him.

"Look," he said to Jack. "See the gallows? Spend the night under it. By morning you'll know what shivering is."

"Thank you, thank you," said Jack, and made himself comfortable under the gallows. The air was cool, so he kindled a fire. Looking up, he felt sorry for the two corpses dangling in the wind. "Hey, you two, come down," he said. "The fire is warm enough for all of us."

The corpses remained silent, so Jack climbed up and cut them loose. He sat them upright by the blaze and talked to them, but they only stared into the night. "With company like this, it's best to go to sleep," said Jack. He yawned and closed his eyes.

The next morning the man came back to see if Jack had found out what shivering is. "Shivering, no," said Jack. "Boredom, yes." The man shook his head, then he said, "Try the haunted castle in the next town."

Jack found the castle and went to the king.

"I have been told that I might learn to shiver in your castle," Jack said.

The king looked at him with sad eyes. "Yes," he said, "this is the right place. An evil spirit has put my daughter to sleep. He who can spend three nights in a row in this haunted castle shall set her free. Many have tried, but they have all died. Go away. You are so young."

"No," said Jack. "I'll stay."

On the first night Jack was sitting alone by the hearth when a cat with two heads jumped out of the fire and asked him if he would play cards. "Good idea," said Jack, but the cat jumped at him to scratch out his eyes. Jack grabbed her by the tail and threw her out the window, then he went to bed. Suddenly the bed began to move. Faster and faster it galloped, down the hallway, up the stairs, across the rooms, through the cellar and attic, and finally back to Jack's room.

"What fun," said Jack, "more, more," but the bed seemed tired, and Jack himself soon fell asleep.

In the morning the king came and was astonished, but still very glad, to find that Jack was alive. "It's no use," said Jack, "I'll never learn how to shiver."

On the second night he was sitting by the fireplace when he heard a great howling and screaming. The door opened slowly, making hardly any noise as the top half of a monster moved in through the air. The monster cried and belched and moaned, and the door shut with a bang.

"Poor thing," said Jack. "It must be terribly uncomfortable to have no legs to stand on." The door opened again and the monster's lower half came bouncing in. "That's better," said Jack as the two halves fitted together to make one whole monster.

"What can I do for you?" asked Jack. Just then the door swung open again and many more halves, three-quarters, and quarters came floating in. All the pieces put themselves together, fitting like jigsaw puzzles into a whole band of monsters. They were all ugly and their breath smelled horrible.

"Would anyone care for some bowling?" asked one of them. He pulled out a skull for a bowling ball and some bleached bones for pins. Jack and the monsters were bowling and having a fine time when the clock struck twelve. At once the monsters fell apart into pieces again.

"And let's take him with us," said one of them, pointing to Jack.

"Oh no, you don't," said Jack. He took a burning log from the fireplace and rushed at them with it. If there is anything monsters hate, it is fire. They all fled into the night, and Jack went to sleep.

In the morning the king came and was happy to find Jack still alive. "How was last night?" he asked.

"Splendid," said Jack. "I had a fine bowling game with some monsters and enjoyed myself very much."

"Were you afraid? Did you shiver?" asked the king.

"No," said Jack. "I don't think I'll ever learn."

On the third night Jack was sitting by his fireplace and wondering if he would ever learn to shiver. Suddenly six men came in, carrying a coffin. They put it down and went out without saying a word.

"Ah, that must be my cousin who died not long ago," said Jack, and opened the coffin. Inside was a corpse, all cold and white. "No need to be so cold, my dear friend," said Jack. He lifted the body out, and put it near the fire. Then he rubbed its icy hands, but they stayed as cold as ever.

When it was time to sleep, he put the dead man in the bed beside himself hoping to warm him. Soon Jack fell asleep. In the middle of the night he felt someone tap his shoulder. It was the corpse.

"I'm glad you're alive again," said Jack sleepily. "What is it?"

The corpse said, "I must drink your blood now."

"My blood? My foot!" said Jack, seizing the corpse and putting him back in the coffin. "This will teach you to be more grateful," said Jack, and he nailed the coffin shut. At that, the six men came in and carried it out as silently as they had brought it in.

"Oh, poor me," said Jack. "I'll never learn to shiver." He had scarcely spoken when he heard a knock at the door. In walked a giant with a long, white beard. He looked very old.

"Now you will learn what shivering means," said the giant. "You are about to die."

"That's not very likely," said Jack. "You may be bigger than I, but you are not stronger."

"We shall see," said the giant, and he led Jack through a dark tunnel to the royal blacksmith shop. There he took a sledgehammer and hit a heavy anvil so hard that it sank into the ground.

"I can do better than that," said Jack. He picked up an ax and went to another anvil. The old giant bent forward to watch, with his beard hanging down. Jack raised the ax and with one mighty blow split the anvil, wedging the beard in between the halves.

"Now I have you," said Jack, and he began to beat the old giant with a stick.

"Let me go," begged the giant, "and I will show you the treasures of this castle."

Jack freed the giant's beard, and the old man led him to the cellar of the castle. He showed Jack three chests full of gold. "One chest is for the king, one is for the poor, and the third belongs to you," he said.

Just then the clock struck twelve and the old giant disappeared. Jack found his way along the dark stairways and hallways until he came to his room. He climbed into bed and went to sleep.

In the morning the king came. "What happened last night? Have you learned to shiver?" he asked Jack.

"Last night my dead cousin came to visit me, and an old giant showed me some chests of gold in the cellar, but no one showed me how to shiver," said Jack.

"Bless you. Three nights have passed and you have broken the evil spell and freed my beautiful daughter," said the king. "I will introduce you to her."

When Jack and the princess met they fell in love and wanted to become man and wife. The king was pleased. The gold was fetched from the cellar and the marriage was celebrated with great joy.

Pleased as Jack was to be a prince and to have such a lovely wife, one thing still bothered him. "Oh, if I only knew how to shiver, my happiness would be complete," he kept saying.

At last the princess thought of a way to solve the problem. One afternoon she dipped a pail into the brook that flowed through the castle garden. When she drew it up, it was full of lively little minnows swimming about.

That night, when Jack was asleep, the princess drew back the sheets and poured the pailful of small silvery fish all over him. Jack jumped up when he felt the minnows slithering against his skin. Laughing with joy, he cried, "I'm shivering . . . I'm shivering . . . at last I know what shivering is!"

The Seven Swabians

There were once seven Swabians who went out to see the world
hoping for adventure and the chance to perform brave deeds.
For protection they took just one long spear. After days of
marching, at last they had their chance. In the middle of a
field, they saw a creature sitting with its big eyes wide open and
its big ears pricked up. The Swabians had never seen a rabbit
before and they thought it was a monster. They lined up along
their spear when fear overcame them. Instead of attacking,
they cried for mercy:

Only the small Swabian, at the end of the spear's handle, kept pushing — he could not see the rabbit. The others fled in all directions to hide, and the rabbit ran away. When the Swabians thought things safe, they crept out of hiding.

They lined up grasping their spear and started marching again. Soon they came to a wide river. There was no bridge across it and there were no boats. A man was working on the

other side, and the Swabians called to him, "How can we get across?" He did not understand them, so he called back, "What? What?"

The Swabians thought he was saying, "Wade. Wade." So the leader walked into the water, followed by the other Swabians, each in his place, marching left right, left right, into the river — all except the little one at the end. As usual, he was not paying attention. The six valiant Swabians soon sank to the bottom. When the smallest Swabian saw the leader's hat bobbing along the river, he knew that something was wrong, and returned home to tell this story.

Folk tales have always been reinterpreted and amplified in their passage from mouth to mouth and culture to culture. In retelling the Grimm stories in this collection, Eric Carle has introduced his own variations. After reading the original Grimm texts as well as those of such folklorists as Andrew Lang and Ludwig Bechstein, Mr. Carle decided to write his own versions. They are based partly on childhood memory and grow from the author's belief that folk and fairy tales should continue to grow and change with the times. The great work of the Grimm brothers is clearly invaluable; they committed to print — and thus preserved — a living art form that might otherwise have been lost to us. Still, folklore continues to evolve. As both storyteller and illustrator, Eric Carle has achieved a compelling unity of effect that captures the homely wisdom, fantasy, and humor of these childhood favorites.

Born in the United States, Eric Carle was brought up in Germany, where he studied at the Akademie der bildenden Kunst in Stuttgart. He has written and illustrated many picture books that are enjoyed by children throughout the world. Mr. Carle now lives in Massachusetts.